For Amelia and David

Library of Congress Cataloging-in-Publication Data

Benson, Patrick. Little penguin
Summary: Comparing herself to the larger Emperor penguins,
Pip the Adélie penguin feels unhappy with her size until an
encounter with a huge sperm whale puts things in perspective for her.
[1. Adélie penguin—Fiction.   2. Emperor penguin—Fiction.
3. Penguins—Fiction.   4. Size—Fiction.]
I. Title. PZ7.B44735Li 1991   [E]   90-7101
ISBN 0-399-21757-6
First impression

LITTLE PENGUIN

PATRICK BENSON

Philomel Books
New York

<big>H</big>ere's Pip –

who lives in the Antarctic.

She's an Adélie penguin

and she's three years old.

Pip often goes exploring.

Here she is, walking past

some other penguins. These
are Emperor penguins who
also live in the Antarctic.

Some of them are three
too, but they're all much
bigger than Pip.

"Why am I a little penguin?" Pip wondered, as she walked up a snow-covered hill.

"Why aren't I a big penguin?" she wondered, as she tobogganed back down.

WHUMPH!

Pip went

head first into

a snowdrift.

I'm a little penguin, I am three,

sang Pip, as she skated

over the ice.

WHUMPH!

She did a
somersault and
landed upside down.

I'm a little penguin by the sea,

sang Pip, as she came

to the edge of the ice.

She jumped into

the sea and landed

with an enormous …

SPLASH!

"Why are some fish little?"
wondered Pip, as she dived
deep down.

"Why are some fish big?" she wondered, as she shot back up.

I'm a little penguin, look at me, sang Pip, as she swam past something huge and black.

Pip jumped ...

on to the huge black thing.

She slipped and tumbled.

SPLASH!

I spy with my little eye, thought Pip, as she plunged

through the clear, bright water.

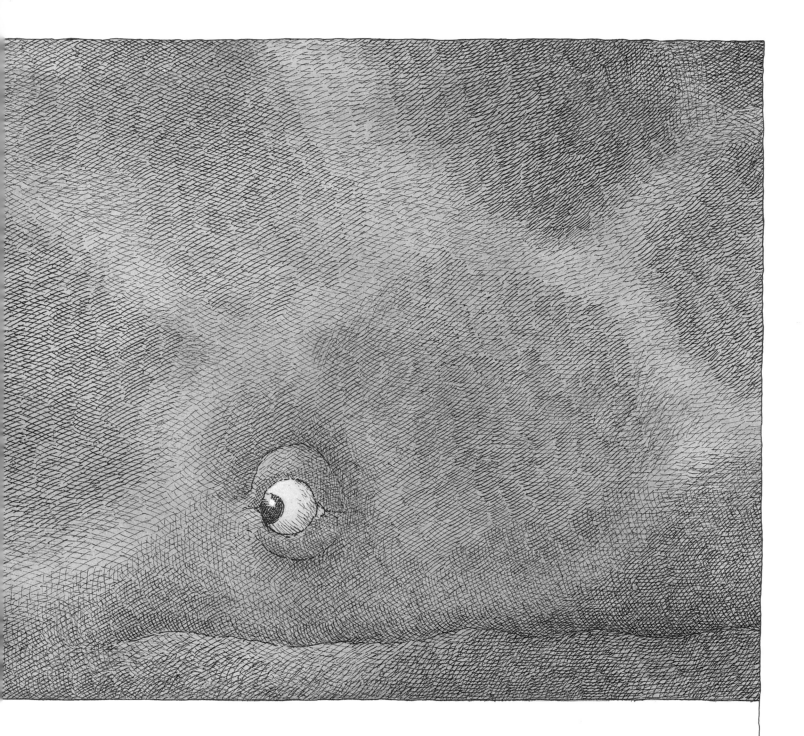

And what she spied was another eye,

spying back at her.

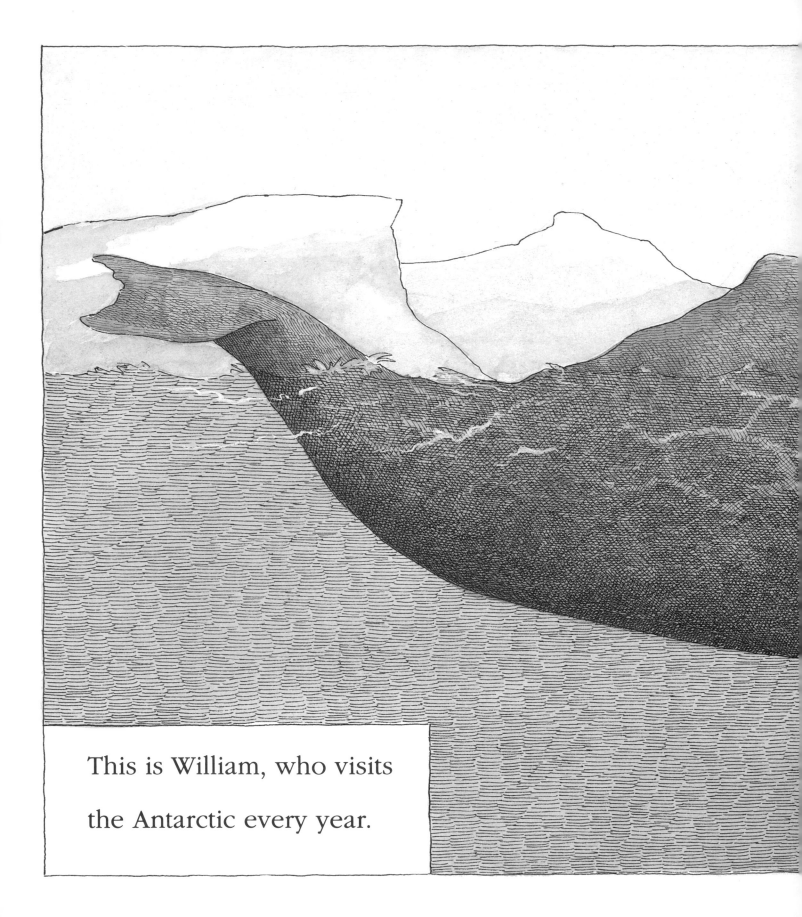

This is William, who visits

the Antarctic every year.

He's a Sperm whale and

he's three years old, too.

Pip and William played together

and as they played, Pip sang:

I'm a little penguin by the sea,

I love you and you love me.

One is one and two is two,

You love me and I love you.

Pip's an Adélie penguin. She lives in the Antarctic and she's three years old.

On her way home, she walks past the Emperor penguins again.

HUMPH!

They're big,

but not so big, she thinks,

and she walks right on by.